Written and illustrated by

DAHLOV IPCAR

LOBSTERMAN

ISBN 0-89272-032-8

9

Down East Books, P.O. Box 679, Camden, ME 04843

For all the fishermen's children of
Georgetown, Maine

Larry lives in a fishing village on the coast of Maine. White gulls soar above his house and perch on the roof top. From his window he can see the harbor full of fishing boats.

There are long wharves with derricks for unloading the fish. Big boats and little boats are tied up to moorings. There are trim, white lobster boats and big sardine carriers; and draggers with fish nets drooping from their masts and big, round, rusty floats dangling at their sides. There are sailboats, and motorboats, and dinghies, and dories.

Larry's father is a lobster fisherman and owns one of the lobster boats. He fishes for lobsters all year round, even in the winter, if weather permits. But winter storms are hard on boats and traps, so at least once a year a lobsterman has to overhaul his gear. Every spring Larry's father has his big boat hauled out of the water, and then he and Larry work on her.

They scrape off the old paint and sand her smooth and caulk her seams. Then they give her a brand new coat of paint. They paint her deck yellow, and her hull white with a black stripe and red below the waterline.

They paint their lobster trap buoys too in the spring. Larry's father paints his buoys red and yellow and black. Every lobsterman uses different colors so that he can tell his buoys from the others.

All over town the sides of the sheds are covered with newly painted buoys hanging up to dry. And everywhere lobster traps are piled up high on the wharves and in the yards.

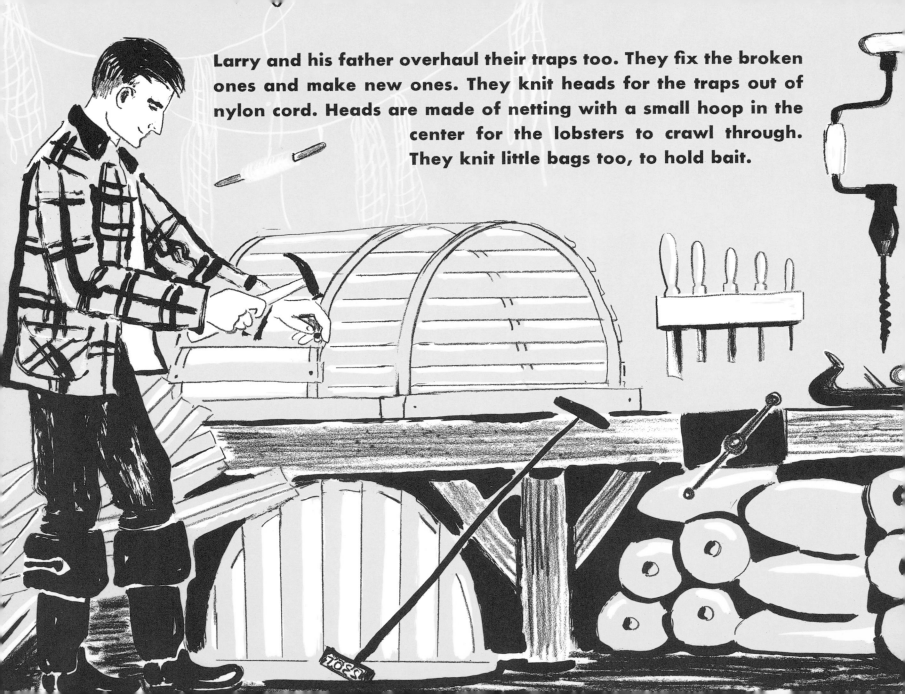

Larry and his father overhaul their traps too. They fix the broken ones and make new ones. They knit heads for the traps out of nylon cord. Heads are made of netting with a small hoop in the center for the lobsters to crawl through. They knit little bags too, to hold bait.

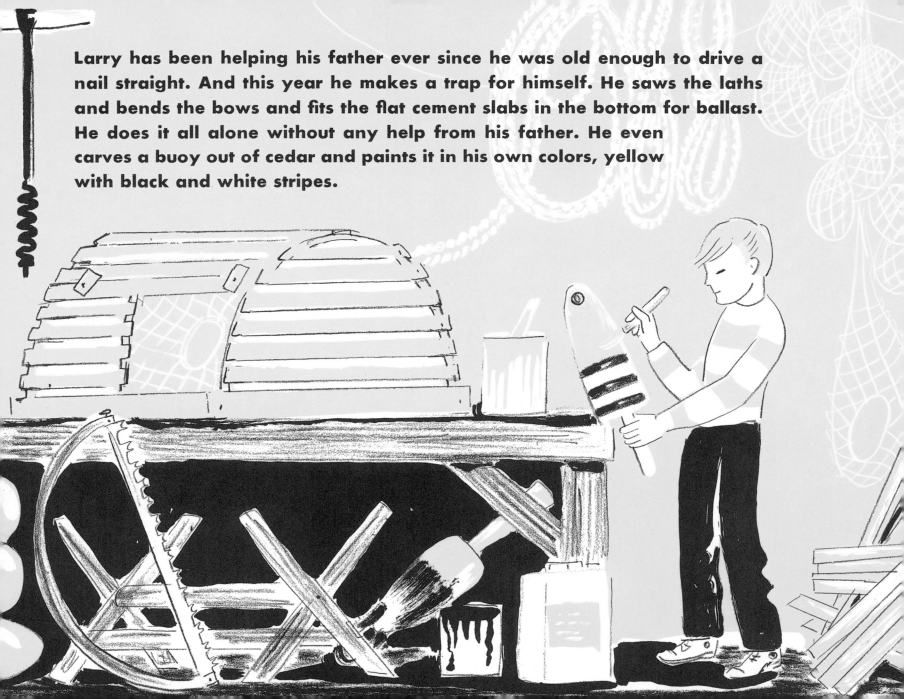

Larry has been helping his father ever since he was old enough to drive a nail straight. And this year he makes a trap for himself. He saws the laths and bends the bows and fits the flat cement slabs in the bottom for ballast. He does it all alone without any help from his father. He even carves a buoy out of cedar and paints it in his own colors, yellow with black and white stripes.

Soon everything is ready. One morning early in May they make their first trip out to set their traps. It is still dark when they eat breakfast and put on their yellow waterproof pants and jackets and their black hip boots. Larry helps his father carry the gear down to the dock. There they load the big boat with as many traps as she can carry. Then Larry's father starts the engine, and they chug out of the harbor.

They chug past the big black buoy that marks the channel and past the tall spindle that marks hidden rocks under water.

White gulls fly after them, and black cormorants dive into the water and swim beside them with only their heads and necks showing.

They see a big sardine carrier alongside a weir taking herring on board, pumping them up through a big hose into the hold. The hose hangs over the top of the weir into the water where the fish have been caught inside the big circle of posts lined with nets.

Larry's father stops his boat and buys a couple of bushels of herring to use for bait in his lobster traps.

They pass beaches where clamdiggers are digging for clams. They pass rocky islands where seals bask in the sun with their babies. Some of them dive into the water and swim after the boat with only their heads showing above the water. Larry throws a herring to one of them and she catches it.

Then Larry takes the wheel while his father pushes the traps overboard. The lobsters hide deep in the cool, green water among the seaweeds and rocks. They hide there with their long feelers waving and their big claws ready to catch any fishes that swim by.

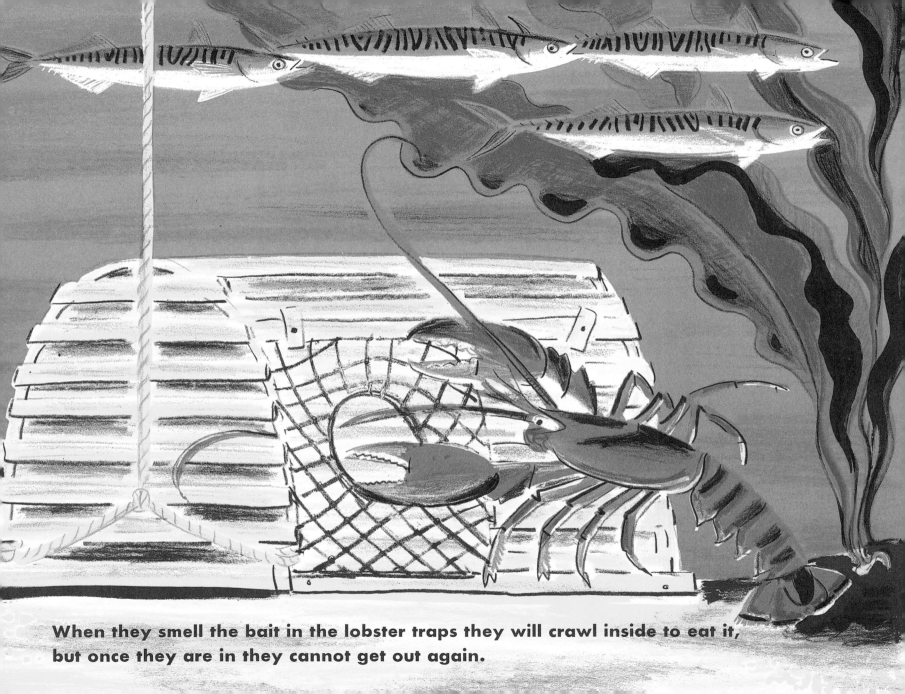

When they smell the bait in the lobster traps they will crawl inside to eat it,
but once they are in they cannot get out again.

Larry and his father come to a little cove where long streamers of brown kelp grow so thick that they can look down and see them waving in a great, dark tangle, like a jungle under the water.

"There must be lobsters down there, for sure," Larry says. "This is where I want to set <u>my</u> trap."

They push his trap over . . . and down it goes, down, down, down, until it disappears among the kelp . . . and only the yellow buoy with black and white stripes floats on top to mark where the trap is.

They set each trap in a different place. They make many trips back to shore for more traps. All day long they drop the traps over the side of the boat, one by one. Some they drop far out to sea and some along the rocky shores. Then as darkness falls over the water they head back home.

Next morning Larry and his father go out in the boat again, this time to haul their traps. Larry reaches over with the gaff and hooks each buoy out of the water.

His father fastens the line to the winch that pulls up the traps. The traps come up over the side, all dripping wet and covered with seaweed. There are starfish and sea urchins and little snails clinging to them. Larry's father opens the door on the side of each trap, and takes out the lobsters. He plugs their claws with a small wooden wedge so they cannot bite each other and throws them in a basket. Then Larry refills the bait bags and they heave the trap overboard again.

LUCILLE

When they pull up Larry's trap out of the tangled kelp, they find three big lobsters in it. They weigh Larry's lobsters and one is a whopping four-pounder, the biggest they have caught so far.

"We'll keep track of all the lobsters you catch," his father says. "Then when we sell them I'll put aside the money for you, and by the end of the summer you ought to have enough to buy something you want. Maybe you can save up for a skiff or an outboard motor."

"But let's not sell these three lobsters," Larry says. "I want to have one for supper tonight, and you and Momma can eat the other two, because they're the first lobsters I ever caught in a trap of my own."

Then Larry puts his lobsters in a pail by themselves so he will know they are his.

When they come back to the harbor Larry's father puts all the lobsters he has caught in a lobster car – a huge crate that floats under water.

He dumps in some mussels for them to eat. When he has enough lobsters in the car he will sell them to a dealer.

But Larry carries his three lobsters home, and his mother cooks them in a big pot until they turn a nice bright red all over. Larry eats every bit of that big lobster all by himself, because he is so hungry. There is nothing that tastes as good as a hot, boiled lobster after a long day at sea.

And when Larry climbs into bed that night he lies awake a while. He thinks about all the many different kinds of fishing, and he says to himself, "I could fish with nets for herring or mackerel, I could work on a big dragger catching redfish or flounder or haddock, I could be a tuna fisherman, or even a clamdigger; but of all the kinds of fishing there are, I think lobstering is the most fun . . . and besides I <u>like</u> lobsters, so I'm going to be a lobsterman when I grow up!"